Finn Throws a Fit!

David Elliott

illustrated by Timothy Basil Ering

WALKER BOOKS
AND SUBSIDIARIES
LONDON · BOSTON · SYDNEY · AUCKLAND

Finn likes peaches.

Usually.

But today Finn doesn't like peaches.
Today Finn doesn't like anything.

Today Finn is grumpy.
Anything could happen.

Uh-oh!
Thunder in the nursery!

FINN THROWS A FIT!

He cries.

The house floods.

He screams.
Look out! Avalanche!

He kicks.
An earthquake shakes the world.

Tidal waves sweep through the living room.

Hurricanes rage in the dining room.

Blizzards blow in the bathroom.

The FIT goes on and on.

It lasts until it doesn't.

The water dries up.
The wind dies down.
The snow melts.

Ahhhhhh!

What was wrong anyway?

He'd like those peaches now.

Please.

To F. H., Zero to Sixty

D. E.

To Mom and Dad, I know that I too threw a tiny fit once
or twice. To Jen, a super mom and wife. And, of course,
cheers to Finn, my talented son. May all that energy that
you have take you to the most amazing places!

T. B. E.

First published 2009 by Walker Books Ltd
87 Vauxhall Walk, London SE11 5HJ

10 9 8 7 6 5 4 3 2 1

Text © 2009 David Elliott
Illustrations © 2009 Timothy Basil Ering

The right of David Elliott and Timothy Basil Ering
to be identified as author and illustrator respectively
of this work has been asserted by them in accordance
with the Copyright, Designs and Patents Act 1988

This book has been typeset in Zalderdash.

Printed in China

British Library Cataloguing in Publication
Data: a catalogue record for this book is available
from the British Library

ISBN 978-1-4063- 2254-5

www.walker.co.uk

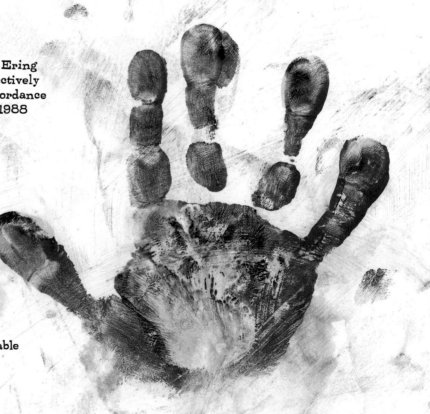